"A dark maze of the soul and mirror eyes that kill: horror at its mythological best."

Seb Doubinsky,
Author of *Omega Gray* and *Goodbye Babylon*

GORGONAEON is a fragmentary and hallucinogenic reading experience. Frequent shifts in time and perspective imbue its scenes with an atmosphere of paranoia and dread, but an optimistic and magical aura can be exhumed from the alchemical wordplay.

Decapitated heads on dining room tables, broken mirrors reflecting things better left unseen, mysterious ladders, plastic bags filled with snakes, decaying gardens, Polaroids of horrified faces in motel rooms, and doll heads filled with blood are poetically stitched to an odd narrative about mental and moral disintegration to create a curious doubling effect.

GORGONAEON is a challenging yet rewarding read that will appeal to fans of grotesque surrealism.

"Jordan Krall's Gorgonaeon is a masterful, episodic psychological foray into the existential dread wrought by familial dysfunction, shot through with allusions to Borges' shattered mirror reflections that both distort and express keen truths, and Ballard's crisp, cool (icy, but Krall is more intimate) stylings. The inverted Escheresque scene-construction opens as venom spat from the mouths of Medusa's heinous headdress, before slowly dissolving into the grey matter nightmare of disorientation and madness...or is this an unflinching reality we'd rather ignore honed to shocking, pristine perfection? Thought-provoking, mind-bending, and rather brilliant."

John Claude Smith,
Author of *Riding the Centipede* and *Autumn in the Abyss*

GORGONAEON

Jordan Krall

DUNHAMS MANOR PRESS

Dunwich – East Brunswick – Fisherville

Published by **Dunhams Manor Press**
An imprint of **Dynatox Ministries**
This is the 2nd paperback edition.
Revised with new material.

© 2015 Jordan Krall

Cover by Jordan Krall

Dunhams Manor Press
East Brunswick, New Jersey
USA

www.dunhamsmanor.com

ACKNOWLEDGEMENTS

Dave Felton, Christopher Slatsky, Dana Krall,
Joe Zanetti, Philip LoPresti, Jon Padgett,
Thomas Ligotti, Seb Doubinsky, Michael Nau,
Clint Leugner, Christopher Ropes, Christopher Bruno,
Matt Bialer, Chris Mihal, Antonio Magogoli.

....mother?

You enter the house through the side door. Instead of taking the stairs to the cellar, you take the steps up to the main floor. There you find the decapitated heads that are set on the dining room table. You take a seat at the head of the table and you wait. You wait for me to come home. But I may never come home. How does this make you feel?

Somewhere there's a mirror smashed at the foot of a ladder. The ladder is leaning against a house, a house that hasn't been lived in for several years despite the persistent efforts of the real estate agent. The shards of glass at the bottom of the ladder have become stained from bird feces and rust-flavored rain. They have ceased to reflect the sunlight. Now they are simply pieces of something else. I put my hands on the ladder and get ready to climb.

At some level, Philip understands that he is incapable of understanding the lecture but stays nonetheless. He may have many faults but the inclination to quit is not one of them. Two hours into the lecture, Philip's eyes are focused on a shiny piece of metal that is hanging off the edge of the speaker's podium. The words spoken by the lecturer coalesce into memory-speech. Philip does not know if the words he is processing are real, imaginary, or some combination of the two. In his notepad, he scribbles down as many of the sounds as possible until the point on the pencil silently breaks. He does not have another pencil.

May 29, 198X

Dear Philip,

Greetings from Brunswick! We miss you, both of us. In fact, Diana said she owes you a big kiss the next time she sees you. I suggest you take her up on that offer! She's not one to take no for an answer.

You had mentioned in your last letter your new position as head of research-and-development at that new company that opened in the industrial park near your house (the name of the company escapes me and I do not have your letter handy. I apologize.) I was wondering how that was going. Please be sure to tell me all about it in your next letter.

I also wanted to share some news myself. Remember I told you I was planning on organizing a small gathering of local poets for a meeting of the minds, an event to contribute to the momentum of the arts in this community? Well, I've done it! At least, I planned it. It is happening two weeks from the date of this letter. I rented out a beautiful Victorian-era house in the center of town. You are, of course, invited. I'd love for you to join us if you are able to leave your job for a few days. Please do let me know either way.

Diana also told me to tell you to give our love to your mother. We were sorry to hear about her illness. Our prayers are with her and you as well.

Your friend,

Apart from sexual attraction, she and I have nothing between us. Maybe that's for the best. We make love, we smoke, we say goodbye. That has worked for the last year. I don't even know where she lives. We always meet at my apartment which I'm fine with since I loathe leaving the house anyway. It's a fine arrangement thus far. Still, I cannot help feeling like she has invested something more in our relationship as if she thinks of us as something other than habitual sexual partners. She hasn't said anything to allude to this fact, though. It's something I recently started feeling during our last few meetings. Then I found that picture of me in her purse. I wasn't snooping, mind you; I had been rummaging around in there looking for cigarettes. I don't even know where she had gotten the picture. It was one taken years ago when I was younger, thinner, and had more hair. The picture made me wonder why she chose to make love to me *now* considering I'm considerably less attractive than I am in that picture. Was she fantasizing about that version of me? I didn't ask her about the picture. I simply put it back where I found it and said nothing when she came back from the bathroom.

Along the side of Highway 18, near the exit to the city of Freehold, someone left a plastic bag filled with dead snakes. Some were garter snakes, some were corn snakes, and there was one eastern milk snake. None were rare or special in any way. But they were all dead and stuffed in a plastic bag on the side of Route 18 near the exit to the city of Freehold.

You've listened to the audio cassettes left by your predecessor. You wonder what compelled a woman of sixty to record nearly a hundred hours of seemingly unimportant monologues. You find it rather interesting. You have always found the mundane details of others fascinating. You live a humdrum life and you cherish the monotony of normality especially when it means you can be an observer instead of a participant. You like to watch. You've always liked to watch, ever since you were a little girl. Your mother scolded you often because of this habit. It is a mirror to your own life. You are listening to the audio cassettes now. Your predecessor has decided she no longer wants to tend to her garden and that she will let the weeds take it all. She is quite poetic about it, using exotic vocabulary to create a vivid picture of the gradual destruction of her once precious garden. She describes the rotting vegetation that will engulf it. She sounds as if she holds the future rot in reverence, as if her religion is not one of spirituality but of the worship of such vegetative death. You listen and decide you will grow a garden of your own.

There are several motels along the highway. None of them are associated with any franchise. Each is its own entity and plays by its own rules. It appears, from the outside, that these motels have not been remodeled in at least three decades. This is not to say they are in any state of disrepair (aside from the occasional broken shingle or patch of dull paint which, if being honest, cannot be helped). They've managed to stay more or less intact despite the years. On the inside, however… well, I myself have never been inside any of these motels but I've sent friends (or maybe a better word would be 'acquaintances') in to take photographs of the rooms, vending and ice machines, as well as the small office/lobby areas. Over the course of three years I've managed to document approximately seventy-five percent of the motel rooms in the twelve motels along that stretch of highway. I have arranged the photographs (and drawings, since I also hired an artist to draw lifelike sketches of the rooms) in a sort of geo-architectural reproduction of the highway motels. Luckily I have room in my basement for such a project. My husband allowed me full reign over the space despite our original agreement that the basement be his home office. And for that I am grateful. This is an important project.

Philip is careful not to step on any of the flowers as he sneaks through the garden, tip-toeing gracefully. He feels weightless. Is it the pills or the flower stem he has ingested? What a curious question, what a curious dilemma. What is the cause of this sensation and can it be repeated? He reaches the end of the garden and looks up at the moon. There's a face in the moon, a woman's face. Moonbeams shoot out like startled snakes and Philip basks in the serpent glow.

You are surprised at the lack of modern décor in my home. You should have realized by now I've reached the point in my life where I can no longer register color and spatial relationships the way most people do. Because of this, I have kept things the way they were for so many years. Change is unnecessary in my condition and ultimately unethical. You have seen my mother's room, am I correct? You have touched the antiques she had hoarded. You have touched her linens. You have put your nose to her delicates. You are sitting on her bed now, yes? The dusty and expensive bed linens intrigue you. You think you can still see the impression of my mother's body. My mother hasn't been dead for very long but you know that and that's why you are in her room, so you can sniff her residual presence. How long will you stay in my mother's room, on my mother's bed? When will you loosen your grasp on her emeralds? It pains me to acknowledge your pleasure.

She is by far the prettiest girl I've seen around the shop but also the weirdest. She's dressed as if she hadn't used a mirror but had simply taken clothes out of the closet randomly and put them on at a whim. Her apparent eccentricity is confusing. I cannot tell if it's a result of her being artistic or *autistic*. There's a fine line between being aware and unaware of one's own peculiarities. She is looking over at me now... probably because I've been sneaking glances at her for the last fifteen minutes while scribbling in my journal. I imagine I look suspicious. Here I am, a woman old enough to be her mother, observing her, taking notes, wondering about her true nature as a human being sitting in this coffee shop. What does she think of me? I can only guess. She thinks I'm some old hag, a creepy tea-drinking matron. I can't help it. I have compulsions. I am impulsive. But when I start on such a task and I do not waver from it. I will not stop until my journal is filled with observations of my subject. I cannot rely on my eyes or memory anymore so I need to write things down. Sometimes I draw things: stick figures and squiggly lines. I am not an artist but hand drawn images often spark remembrances. I draw the girl, a stick figure clothed in a square, her hair are squiggly lines. When I look at it later, I will remember her deceptive beauty.

Philip begins taking pills on the first of October as his doctor instructed him: one pill twice a day. He is reluctant to take them. He does not trust medicine and does not trust doctors but he makes the decision to overcome his mild paranoia and distrust and begin the prescription. His wife tells him the medicine might make him feel better and less sluggish. She tells him that he is always just *sitting there* like a rock. She has often referred to him as her "inanimate husband" which often made him feel like an automaton in disrepair. Philip tells his wife about his concerns over side effects. She gently dismisses his worries and tells him the side effects, if there are any, will surely be miniscule compared to his general ailment. Philip takes his pill with room temperature water. A minute later he complains of blurred vision. His wife tells him he's being silly and that his vision isn't blurred. Philip looks in the bathroom mirror and sees a man that resembles him but is not him. He shakes his head and is in a wilderness of mirrors. Green lights reflect off all surfaces. Philip is blinded and sees only snakes. After using the toilet, he is back to normal.

On the side of Highway 18 in Old Bridge, there is a certain ditch where one can find plastic bags full of toy snakes. Several years ago, in that very same ditch, the body of seventeen-year-old Nicole Logla was found by a man whose car had broken down on the side of the road. Nicole had been strangled. She had not been sexually assaulted. Her killer was never apprehended. The man who found her was quickly ruled out as a suspect by the local police.

One would think that by entering my home you'd grasp the enormity of my problem, the overwhelming need for conclusions, for the untangling of this philosophical *Rattenkönig*. But one cannot expect the seemingly obvious to occur. One has to assume that Fate is as blind as the rest of the gods, those angry harbingers of entanglement. It is comforting to expect answers, to await them in the tenebrous caves of one's expectant brain matter. But this is not the case now. You enter my house and are clueless as to what to do next. You have wasted your time but most importantly, *you have wasted mine.*

Philip tests the microphone by blowing into it. He startles several elderly women sitting up front. He apologizes and lowers the volume. He starts to speak to the group, going through the routine he rehearsed at home for the last three weeks. He gets through successfully and blushes at the weak applause. He steps out from behind the podium and waits by the table on which there are copies of his newest book, *A Complete History of Industrial Parks.*

There is nothing in the box except for a series of Polaroid pictures. I expected more, to be honest, since the box is so huge and so heavy. It is as if the *air itself* is heavy and once I had opened the box, the weight floated out of it. Each Polaroid picture is of a close-up of a face, features frozen in horror or shock. I put the pictures together like a puzzle but they form nothing of value, at least not that I could see. It is a mess, just nonsense, nothing but glimpses of cheeks, eyes, lips, and grimaces all stuck in place. Why would someone take these pictures? They are useless but I am reluctant to dispose of them. Why do I feel the need to keep these pictures, the ones I found in a box in the closet of my motel room?

Come to me, my child. Embrace me in the presences of She Who Stares. I'll place my lips upon your eyelids and protect you from the glare. You position yourself accordingly. I will lower you into the earth tomorrow. I will worship your dirt.

The motel room is newly cleaned by the housekeeping staff but the perfume smell is still there, lingering in every inch of space. Perfume and bleach mingle along with the ghosts of hundreds of cigarettes. A man is sitting on the edge of the bed, picking at his snakeskin belt. What to do… What to do… He turns on the television and watches an old movie: Technicolor drama about a search for someone known as The Lion. He wants to burn the television. He believes he is the notorious Motel Man, that mythological figure but he is not. He is simply a man in a motel.

They're staring at us. But let them stare. Stare at my wooden visage. Stare at my impotent arms. Their eyes want to burn us but our forms are simply shadows, automatons of ash. I will be lowered into the earth tomorrow but you will not miss me for there is nothing to be missed. Send my regards to your mother.

Philip hears the violin and is lured into the room. On the bed: the flayed body of a multi-limbed sacrifice. Violins penetrate the womb and Philip sits on the edge of the bed and caresses the body until it disappears in to the glassy walls of the motel room.

The man cleans up the shards of glass. The mirrors have been broken but he vows to piece them together and use them in his films. Reflections make great actors and actresses. He hopes to film hours and hours of an epic feature to be shown to the local Film Studies Club. He believes the film will impress the members enough to convince them to finance his next project: a 24-hour cinematic study of ugliness in the form of doomed reflections. What beauty is there in one's true reflection? Your countenance is all wrong. Blame the glass. You crawl out of the earth tomorrow.

To comprehend the interpretations of the herald's message, one must assume the identity of the herald *herself* since, because of her origin, she has encoded the message in the very essence of her nature, the cryptic illuminations on the yellowed pages of her person, a touchstone charred by the complexities of her evolution from maiden to herald. To translate such ideas, one must fashion a brain in the tradition of bold projections, those grey matter visions projected onto cave walls, blinking only with the torch light since the lunar gaze does not penetrate that far into the penetralia to her maidenhead. The herald's message will murder the messenger as it has for aeons. To comprehend is to see one's own reflection in the mirrored agony of the herald herself. That's all I have to say on this matter.

Philip splits his lip open with an obsidian blade and lets the wound empty onto the doll's head or, more specifically, the doll's face, a blank stare and gaping mouth now showered in a deep red offering of self-reflection. The incantation bowl is modernized into child's play. Philip wipes his fingers on the mirror and draws a moon in blood. He remembers his mother.

The motel is a labyrinthine hell of squalor, a drug-infested snake-pit inhabited by transient predators armed with archaic lizard-brains fueled by devils both chemical and botanical. This is where I find myself on retreat, a place where I can finally complete my role as scrivener of lurid rituals, a loathsome scribe in a pit-of-horror scriptorium. All of this is utter nonsense to anyone not involved in this hell. I await her message so I can finally put down my pen and close my eyes. Please wipe away the dirt.

Such a brutal account of his mother's death enables Philip to follow through with the photographic documentation of the unsolved murders of the other women. He does not believe this will lead to any sort of resolution but he follows through nonetheless.

Philip,

Please pass on this message to your mother. I did not have a chance to water the garden this week. Please accept my apologies. Work has been utter hell and my own mother has been ill and uncooperative while I tend to her care. Please know that I will be caring for your mother's garden at the soonest possible moment. I will also get rid of the snakes that have infested it. They seem to have possibly made it into the basement as well.

You are sitting in my chair at the dining room table and you drink from *my* cup the wine *my* husband has poured for you. I trust it pleases your palette. I trust it will satisfy your spirits, put them at ease. I trust my husband is treating you well. He has always treated *me* well. Do you realize that I am staring at you? Do you not recognize my gaze?

To find fault in what I did... that's the height of oblivious arrogance on your part. Nothing I have said or done has been miscalculated. My passion speaks for itself. The letters I've sent Philip should attest to that if you have even bothered to read them all word-for-word (I know you read his mail anyway). The fault lies not with *me* but with the emboldened nature of *your humanity*, that horrible burden you have to endure along the ugly path through this hallucinatory maze of divine dread, that aching pit you've decided to surrender to. None of this is my fault and I would like you to know that.

The snakes infested the top floor of the apartment building but none of the lower floors were affected in the least. By the time Animal Control arrived, the snakes had disappeared as suddenly as they had appeared.

Philip burns the pills over the stove. He watches the smoke: an amorphous incarnation of pharmaceutical jinn. He is betraying the doctor's orders. He does not want to fall into the lunar trap, does not want to suckle at the moon's slithering tide, does not want die slowly by starlit corruption. If his wife finds out about the pills, she will become angry and insist he call the doctor. Philip is prepared for the fallout just as long as he no longer has to visit the garden in the presence of the jinn.

This particular motel was designed as a series of zig-zags. Seen from above, it resembles several short bolts of lightning. Since its construction in 196X, the motel has seen no fewer than five owners and as many remodelings. Located behind the motel is a small garden where the third owner used to grow fresh fruits and vegetables. It is now covered with weeds and infested with snakes and pests.

Philip shows up late for work. His manager confronts him as soon as he walks through the door. The manager is trying to be as benevolent as possible while explaining to Philip that his tardiness has cost the company several sales. The losses aren't actually directly related to Philip's lateness... but rather indirectly, as some distant domino down the line, splitting off into a pattern of sale-resale, profit margin, and cost effectiveness meetings. The business has recently splintered off into various subsidiaries and each of them has birthed its own group of subsidiaries and so on. Philip does not know exactly which of the subsidiaries he has indirectly affected by his late arrival. He manager, however, assures him it was an unnecessary and substantial loss. Philip apologizes and the manager accepts it with a tight-mouthed smile and nodding of his balding head. He tells Philip to stay an extra hour to make up for his mistake. Philip reluctantly agrees.

You dig in my backyard with the silver spoons bequeathed to you by your grandmother. You love digging in the soil, the rich blackness with the curling insects, the occasional piece of rotted vegetation. I do not know your goal but I know you have been diligent in your seeking. I respect that. I even admire it. You have taken leave of your job to spend your days in my backyard, digging with spoons, fingering the dirt, becoming intimate with the earth. I allow you to do this because… well, because there's no reason why I *shouldn't*. I have no use of my backyard. My gardening days are over. I have no children and therefore, no grandchildren. No nieces or nephews. In fact, as you know, I've never taken a husband and never considered adopting a child on my own. After all, what do I have to offer a child? I have no pets, no dog to run in the yard, no need to nurture another human being. So it is no concern of mine if you want to explore the ground, *my* ground, the property I inherited from my father after he passed, after many years of his being paralyzed, stone-like, from a mysterious illness no doctor could diagnose. I'm sure if he were alive today, he would not mind your digging. In fact, he would probably find it amusing. He always found joy in such small, meaningless endeavors.

The strangulation occurred… Foreign object, a belt, something coiled around his neck, the whispering of solemn curses, a hiss of fading breath, the hiss of stolen secrets pushed forth by lungs untouched by impurity, hush, hush, my secret beauty, I will investigate further, I promise you.

In the motel room, the artist lifts her arms and tries touching the water-stained ceiling. She is two inches too short even on her tippy-toes. The artist sits down on the carpet, fingering the coarse fibers, the crumbs, the remnants of guests far gone. She puts her fingers to her nose, smells them: musty warmth and spoiled food stench. She inhabits the space between ceiling and floor, amassing small wounds across her fingertips which she pretends are paint brushes. She paints the air in between the walls and watches green spirals degenerate into dead blossoms at her feet. She fingers her very own rotting garden.

I find myself bothered by hints of some clandestine machination that harbors all my future thoughts. I cannot plan for the future because my husband tells me that everything is all set, arranged and that I need not worry about a thing. But there are so many things in competition for my attention and for my nerves. He thinks I'm a fool, a helpless weakling. But I am not. I will control more things in my life than he will ever wish to control. I just need more time and I need to separate myself, isolate myself, so these hints of some clandestine machination does not tempt me into passive oblivion.

I always wanted to be an artist ever since I was a child. My mother used to paint, not professionally, but often enough that she got quite good and received many compliments from strangers who managed to stumble into our home (my mother often entertained salesman and other solicitors much to my father's dismay). Several of her paintings were also displayed at our town's small library, an honor that both pleased and embarrassed my mother. She did not encourage my artistic pursuits, however. Quite the opposite. She would not let me near her paints and other supplies. There were times I snuck into her studio (our basement) and scoop miniscule amounts of paint into small baby food jars, eventually collecting enough to paint my first picture. I had no real canvas but instead used a piece of cardboard ten inches by eight inches. With an insufficient set of materials, I created a landscape of childish and mythological doom: a woman (who I now realize resembles my mother, something I was not conscious of at the time) among a horde of skeletal but gorgeous creatures. The woman, sword in hand, was in mid-decapitation of one of the attackers. Above her were the moon and one star. I ran out of paint before I could fill the sky with other celestial bodies. I kept the painting a secret from everyone except my younger brother Philip. When he was thirteen, I showed it to him. At first, he laughed at it but once he perused it enough, he became angry. He told me to put it away, that it was an evil picture. From that moment on, I have showed no person any of my six hundred and fourteen paintings.

Philip leans out his bedroom window and scatters the bone dust over the garden. Some of it is carried off in the breeze but most of it lands in the soil and on the leaves of the plants and on the flower petals. Philip leans back in, closes the window and kneels on the floor, facing the eastern wall of his room. On that wall there are several pages thumb-tacked. These pages had been removed from library books and depict various diagrams, illustrations, and photographs that Philip has been obsessed with for several years, ever since his mother's death. The limits of his intestinal fortitude are being tested.

Within the text, one finds a common theme. The theme is not evident when read silently to oneself. The words must be read aloud, reciting as if from a play though the text is not a play. The text has no dialogue and no characters, no sequence of events. There is no ending despite the words at the end of the text that say **THE END** in bold black letters.

After pulling the rope, you realize it is attached only to a manikin head that is nailed to the highest shelf in my mother's bedroom. You can pull the rope again, if you'd like, but I assure you it will not do much good. Where my mother obtained that manikin head, I can only guess and it wouldn't be a good guess at that. It was certainly acquired before my birth. After I was born, she never acquired much in the way of possessions. Maybe she was afraid my presence in the house would lead to the corruption of her things though I'd like to imagine that it was because she felt like she didn't need anything else but me, her only child. I don't know. You continue to explore my mother's room. Is there no end to your curiosity?

The message sent to Philip was disguised as a textual analysis of a XXXXX translation of an XXXXX invocation of a long-forgotten minor deity (thought to have been worshipped sometime between 2500 and 2400 B.C.E.). This unnamed deity is simply mentioned in the text and not described. It is, in Philip's opinion, a proper substitution for a mother figure. But who sent this message?

Despite your pleading, your wailing and gnashing of teeth in my presence, I am reluctant to consider your apology sincere. Whose forgiveness do you desire? Just mine? Is my forgiveness important enough that you would degrade yourself like this? I will tell you right now my forgiveness is no sanctuary. I simply do not care either way. I hold no malice against you, against your mistakes, your offenses, intentional or otherwise. You can leave, go back into the dust, into the swamp, into the cold brittle house of your reluctant self-reliance. I have no need for you. I have no desire to make you whole. Our mother's house is crumbling anyway. Salvage what you can.

The motel room is hot because the air conditioner is broken. The windows are covered with hand prints. The carpet is stained. The television is twenty-years old. The bed is dusty. On the walls hang portraits of strong men posing within dangerous settings. They will all be conquered soon enough. Their strength is no match for time, for the entropy of the motel's walls. Within the walls there are rusted coins, scraps of newspaper, ticket stubs, fishhooks, dull razors, overfed rats, coffee cups, powdered wigs, and ancient snakeskin. The motel room is hot. The walls bubble, the paint eager to escape. The carpet is stained with old milk, maybe blood, baby vomit, maybe semen, other things unknown, long forgotten. The motel room is hot because the air conditioner is broken but no one has bothered to get it fixed despite dozens of complaints from guests.

Philip is nervous today. He blames the caffeine even though it could be the side effects of his discontinuing his medication. He is walking along the highway, fidgeting with the coins in his pocket, trying to decipher the embossed writing on them, wondering if he could somehow translate them into a new language, one that he is creating along with his nervous tics and the anxious tinkering in his brain. Cars speed past on the highway, sending noxious breezes his way. He feels he can die at any moment since the cars are very close. It is possible someone will find his body later. Someone will find his body in pieces. If a car hits him at such a great speed, the metallic impact may very well cut him in two. He is, after all, quite frail. Philip imagines being discovered on the side of the highway. Who will find the body? What will they do? What if he is found by someone with some ghoulish intent? Will his body become fodder for a morbid examination? Will it be photographed? Will the photographs become fetish objects? These thoughts both worry and fascinate him. He takes a step closer to the road, hoping to tempt Fate with his fragile body, an offering to whatever forces lie in wait for such tragic moments of self-realization.

It should be no surprise to you that my opinion of you as a mother is quite low. Up until recently, I thought myself cruel for harboring such a view but, as a close friend explained to me, you are the one who should be ashamed and if you are not, then it is this obliviousness that caused you to be such a terrible beast of a mother. In my last letter, I made myself perfectly clear and aired my grievances plainly and without emotional camouflage. You taught me that, you know, to separate emotion from action. That's probably the only worthwhile thing you've ever passed down to me. Other than that, you have caused me no shortage of unnecessary hurdles both physical and mental. You have wished to create a daughter in your image but instead gave birth to an enemy, one that is always two steps ahead of your psychological nonsense. And nonsense it is! Your last letter, seeking sympathy from me because of several vague medical ailments, was a vomitous joke. How much of a fool do you think I am? You will receive no sympathy from me, no words of comfort or of hope. If there really is a cancer ravaging your insides, my only hope is that it slows its attack and shows no mercy to your monstrous body, that wretched shell that houses your pathetically cruel mind. If I am being too harsh, I do not apologize. I am your daughter but *you*, you are not my mother. Not anymore.

The man is fully covered in armor fashioned from crocodile skin. He is standing in the motel office, obsidian dagger in hand, calling out the names of the stars in his native tongue, a language no longer spoken by anyone other than the man. He moves around the office in a feminine dance, one that requires no music but the sounds in the man's head, the green starlit fires of the mind, the fires that envelop the celestial snakeskin and gives birth to birth itself. The bell on the door sounds and a woman walks into the office. The man drops to his knees and utters a syllable the woman cannot hear. With a movement of the dagger, the man splits open the universe and destroys the afterbirth. The woman does not notice this. She waits for the manager so she could check into a room.

Sounds bother me more than ever. I cannot stand to be in any public place. Sounds coming from multiple sources and multiple directions cradle my brain in thorns. I imagine myself a crucified man, being mocked by sounds, being left to rot from aural decay. An earthquake will crush my mind and turn the sky to black. In my mind, an unending torture, a spiritual revenge against my ancestral cult. I need silence or I will no longer be able to function in the way I need to, in the way that will allow me to complete the task I've given myself and as insignificant as that task might be, it is still my task and I always finish tasks.

Quite frankly, I have more in common with the patients than I do my fellow doctors. That is what my wife told me last night after we had a long discussion about C_____ and T_____. I cannot say this realization is shocking or even disheartening. I imagine there is a logical reason for the similarities, some root cause at the core of our psychological ascent (or *descent* as the case may be). I also think this fact makes me more successful in my doctoring. Even so, I am left to wonder if I am in any danger of acclimating to the standards of some of the patients, of becoming a newly formed version of myself that requires more in the way of psychological upkeep than usual. I am not without my problems but so far these problems have been limited to the mundane. In a way, I fear that I will become an inverted copy of myself, a medicated automaton shuffling about the hospital ward, searching the floor for stray pills and scribbling an exegesis on the walls of the lavatory. I cannot let this become me. This is not out of some idea of self-preservation (after all, what is 'the self' anyway) but because my patients will lose a part of their treatment if they lose me and that is unacceptable to me as a doctor. Because of this, I am going to become more introspective and perform more exploratory surgery upon myself until I find a solution.

And thus she was born, that dreadful infant… Her misshapen head crowned with horsehair and her lips plump with snake venom. No man or woman could look upon that creature and not be sickened. The infant's mother, in her post-partum state, thought the birth a triumphal revelation. To think about the little creature… Oh, I feel sick even imagining its grotesque countenance, its young but wizened form. I've been called upon to be the child's nurse, a *dark interpreter* of sorts. I accepted the job, not without trepidation, because I am in dire need of financial stability and I am never one to shun a challenge. Even so, I'm reluctant to give an account of my experiences because that baby, that creature, is always within eyesight, staring at me…

The man enters into his halcyon coffin, unaided by gods or Fate. He brandishes a knife that had been fashioned by his own hand and sharpened and made strong by starlight, ideal for entering the mouths of snakes. He feels no fear. He swallows the dirt.

Philip tests the microphone by blowing into it. There is nothing in the box except for a series of Polaroid pictures. There are several motels along that highway. A minute later he complains of blurred vision. What beauty is there in one's true reflection? Who will find the body? You have touched her linens. I will control more things in my life than he will ever wish to control. Please pass on this message to your mother. The things that happen in those rooms have been recorded. We will have no solace until the spiral freezes and the scales fall. The spires along the highway will fall.

The man signs the motel ledger, scribbling the name George G. Hensley. He pays in cash for two nights. The clerk tells him the room is out the door and to the left. He can't miss it. The man who signed his name George G. Hensley thanks the clerk and takes his suitcase to his room and starts to unpack until he hears a hissing coming from the bathroom.

It is because of this myth of longsuffering that we have become so comfortable in our positions as bystanders. We have accepted the fact that our actions are unnecessary and ultimately powerless in the barren psychological wasteland that has manifested itself so many years ago when our mother was healthy, when she was, in her own small way, *alive*. I admit I have become a battered witness in the mythical trial, a person unwilling to yield to anger or vengeance. Instead, I have developed my ability to stare directly at the sun, so to speak, and drive my psyche down to tamasic depths which has enabled me to enter the house and not be affected by its lingering miasma of motherhood gone wrong. The entire myth cycle of our upbringing has been documented often enough for me to be comfortable in my role as the 'herald of stability' as I'm often called. Our actions have become fodder for the rumor mill but that is something we have learned to accept, isn't it? Even so, that doesn't make our relationship any easier to mend, now does it?

Philip is sitting on the bed, staring at the static on the motel television. There are flowers beside him. There are also pills. There is noise coming from the television: women's voices discussing life insurance and mascara and shampoo. Philip strains to hear one particular voice, that of a woman who is discussing stonemasonry. He leans forward and cocks an ear toward the speaker. Still, there is only the cacophony of voices that are slithering out with the static. He cannot focus on that woman's voice. He grabs a flower and some pills and throws them at the television. There is a hissing sound behind him and as he turns to face it, his chest tightens. His mother is dead.

I have not witnessed a suitable version of myself in quite some time. Gazing in mirrors, seeking sight through the candle smoke and pharmaceutical haze, I have been chasing after that version of myself that once entered my presence all those years ago, that time when I had been simply a girl and not a woman yet, a girl and not a mother. So I do not know myself even after these hours gazing into black mirrors and white smoke while the curious chemicals make transactions between my cells. The searching may very well be in vain but it's something I cannot abandon for if I do, it would mean the collapse of my womanhood and the dissolution of my sanity.

Yesterday I found a mirror smashed at the foot of a ladder that had been leaning against my mother's house, a house that hasn't been lived in for several years despite the efforts of the real estate agent. The shards of glass at the bottom of the ladder are stained from dog feces. I have gotten some old gardening gloves from the shed and gather the shards of glass. I believe I have them all. If not, then I suppose they will seep into the soil. As for the ladder, I do not know how it got there. For as long as I could remember, it had been in the shed but here it is up against the house, leading up to a window on the second floor, a window whose glass is now shattered, ruined forever like a spinster's bitter maidenhood. Was someone trying to get inside the house? If so, why that window? It isn't very big. It is barely large enough for a small child to enter and even then, it would be a tight fit. But then again, the glass must have been broken from the *inside* since it had landed on the ground. Was something trying to break *out?* And then there is the ladder... If someone had tried breaking out of the house (for whatever reason), how did they get the ladder? But regardless of all this, there is no one living in the house. It had been unoccupied for years, ever since my mother's death. Perhaps I should keep some of the glass. Maybe they contain some clues to this mystery. I don't know. But what I do know is that I am even more uncomfortable entering my mother's house. It is an emptiness I cannot bear.

Philip shouts into the darkness of the motel room and listens for a reply, one that he can easily accept as a conscious doppelganger of his own reluctance to enter the room. The reflection will be hesitant to leave just as he is hesitant to enter. He shouts again, receives no reply, and backs away from the door. Today is not the day for answers.

The bottom rung of the ladder breaks, the wood snapping loudly, louder than expected. The sound echoes through the yard. Dogs bark. A gust of wind blows leaves off the roof of the house. A hornet's nest breaks free from a tree branch and falls to the ground. Glass shatters. A child shouts. Sunlight illuminates the windows. Birds land on the grass. Since the bottom rung is missing now you must take a bigger step to get onto the ladder. Is the rest of the ladder prone to breaking? You cannot tell. Who can tell such a thing? You can only surmise that the chances of your breaking each of the remaining rungs are higher than normal but you are willing to take the risk. Dogs bark. A child cries. Car horns blare. A bicycle chain breaks. You are halfway up the ladder. Your legs are trembling. You want to be weightless. Dogs bark. Your mother's voice in your head saying something about tipping the scales. The hornet's nest is abandoned. A child laughs. Birds land on the roof and peck at the unidentifiable matter caught in the gutter. You are lightheaded now. You hair feels electrified. The sky above you is uneven, incomplete. Your grip loosens. Your legs pull you down. Glass shatters. Sunlight illuminates your body. Dogs bark through the newly settled dirt.

I assume any mispronunciation on your part is due to your lack of practice and not your ignorance of the subject matter. After all, you have always been more knowledgeable than I. The only advantage I hold over you is *time* and that is simply because I choose to live a rather cloistered life despite the myriad opportunities I have been offered to use my knowledge in a more academic manner. That is not something that interests me in the least. Let us leave the classrooms to the innocent lambs and soured instructors, shall we? You and I have always held this same view, that true knowledge, true *insight* is something to be held above any social structure including academia. My advice to you is to practice reciting the words in the darkness of your room, in the silence of isolation, in the coils of your *self.* Those foreign words will soon become like stone in the garden of your intellect. I trust you will be as successful as ever in this endeavor. After all, you've taught me nearly all I know.

I stare at her throughout the day. I believe she has noticed but honestly, I don't care anymore. Let her know my fascination. There are other people here who are complaining about my tendency to stare through meetings instead of moving my eyes in the socially appropriate manner that is expected. That doesn't bother me. Let them talk. Let them complain. Let them discuss me in the privacy of their homes and offices. Let me be the topic of their scandalous conversation as long as I can continue to stare at *her* throughout the day. Nothing else is of any true importance.

Her skin, though smooth and void of blemishes, is cold and gray. She attributes this to years of bathing in milk and using homemade soap. We do not know if this is true but we do not have any reason not to take her at her word. She rarely sleeps and if she does it's only for an hour or two at a time. Her body seems to have moved beyond weariness to the point of hyperawareness. Her eyes are constantly staring, awake and prepared to observe her surroundings. She has no need or desire for dreams. After all, who needs dreams when one lives the life she does?

Philip walks across the highway and into the woods which is really just a gathering of dying and diseased trees. There are hardly any leaves left; it is mostly just bark. These trees, though pathetic, mock Philip as he passes by. He punches one of them, breaking brown shards to the ground. They look like slivers of filthy glass. The trees still mock. They show him exactly what he will soon become. You will be immovable like us. You will be eaten by disease. You will be shunned by all healthy life. Philip scrapes moss off a tree until it is underneath each of his fingernails. He searches the ground for fungus but finds nothing but brittle twigs and snakeskin.

Originally, I thought the crocodile armor to be no more than an apotropaic costume but this thinking was just another example of my usual foolishness. I thought it was simply Pazuzu in an overcoat but my eyes were just another failing aspect of my structure. I cannot believe what I see anymore. Mirrors are useless to me. Nothing has made sense to my vision in years. I pull a knife and stab him in hopes of penetrating that armor but the knife snaps. It is not a knife but only a sliver of glass I must have picked up from the ground at some point. My hand is bleeding now. The blood comes from my palm. There is blood on my groin as well. I need another knife or another piece of glass and maybe I can get through the armor and the overcoat. His teeth are shining in the dark. His eyes reflect the crimson on my hands. I can hear the mewing of creatures hidden in the blackness. My body is giving up. I've been very, very foolish. I've lost too much ground. I'm going to die. If I can just pry the armor off...

A wild boar runs through the parking lot of the motel and several men attempt to capture it. The animal runs out into the highway and is hit by a pickup truck. The wild boar is disemboweled but still alive. The driver of the pickup truck is unconscious as his head has hit the steering wheel upon impact. The men in the parking lot stop and watch the boar drag its body and guts to the other side of the highway into a small patch of woods where it finds a suitable place for the upcoming haruspicy: in a ditch next to the corpse of a middle-aged woman.

During the meeting, several of the poets in attendance complained about the current state of their profession. They complained of the shrinking market for their work and of the lack of respect they experienced from others in the literary world. I listened attentively, nodding my head in a seemingly agreeable manner which is what I've learned to do when faced with habitually whiny people. When their discussion came to an end, I suggested they consider writing prose, if only for a short while, in order to exercise their writing abilities. I was met with a vicious backlash. There was no way *they* were going to change; the world needed to catch up with their artistic prowess in the method they had chosen. I nodded. Finally, the eldest poet among them took leave and the rest of us started discussing something less controversial. From what I recall, the eldest poet who had left first never attended another meeting. I believe he has since died of a snake bite.

You set your course for the heart of the house. You'll never find it. You are not nearly as clever or intuitive as you think you are. You will most likely die before the ruins are unearthed, before the treasure you seek rears its head from its clandestine den. You will die. It is a simple statement of fact: the hallway will consume your suicide just like the highway consumed your mother's. The notion is not preconceived. It is a culmination of much thought, focused and rigorous meditation. You should not be so surprised. I have always been determined in my thinking. I am like a lioness in that regard. Have you checked the attic yet? You probably should not do so. It has never been safe. Not at all. Have you not paid any attention to your mother's lectures? Poor you. I dread the day you find out the truth.

Philip is on the motel room bed. He has an unobstructed view of the bathroom. Inside that room is a pile of old, frayed rope. He had found the rope like that, on the crusted linoleum floor. There are also small piles of dust in the corners of the motel room as if someone had decided to smash stone and leave the remains. Philip has no intention of calling the management. It is out of their hands, out of *his* hands. The placement of everything in the room is as it should be. At some point, everything is where it should be. Otherwise, chaos would consume the very moment of conception.

There have been more murders at that motel than there are rooms there. It was built in 196X and since then there has been an average of a dozen murders a year in and around the motel. Inside the rooms. In the parking lot. In the manager's office. On the back property. Police do not believe the murders are connected.

The woman was crushed with a sledgehammer postmortem, her entire form made practically formless on the damp earth. Several forms of wildlife made home within her dead cells before law enforcement found her corpse. They only stumbled upon it as a result of a much-delayed anonymous tip to the local police department. The case remains unsolved.

The owls inhabiting the attic have made it impossible for us to hold our meetings anywhere in the house. As soon as we enter the house, the animal sounds start. They hoot and flap their wings violently against the walls. From outside, we see their infernal faces, round and ugly, staring at us, mocking us (if these beasts know of such a concept). Our hatred of the owls has grown since the first time we attempted to hold our meetings at the house. At this point, we are nearly ready to enter the attic with weapons to slaughter those invasive pests. But we fear them as much as hate them. None of us will be the first to admit it, though. The only thing I've done is spread talcum powder along the doorway to the attic so those satanic creatures don't venture into the rest of the house. I have used talcum powder against other pests like ants but have no idea if it works on owls, those ugly beasts but we shall see.

Come to me, mother. Embrace me in the presences of She Who Stares. There is not much I can do other than offer you false promises within the light of this cave. The shadows will reconstruct the moment of my birth and the horrific battles of my childhood and yours. I had no idea you used to be an actress. That just goes to show how neglectful of a daughter I have been all these years. I hope someday I can offer some semblance of an apology but as of right now, I'm as emotionless as stone.

From the motel office to my room, it is thirty-five feet. In the room there are bags of party supplies and gag gifts: streamers, banners, noise makers, fake vomit, and rubber snakes. Preparation for the inevitable collapse of normality is necessary for the support of our mental resources. There has not been a celebration in this town for years. I am afraid to admit my family is at least partially to blame for this fact. That being said, it is not so much my fault as it is my responsibility to rectify things in the only way I know and that is in the planning of a replacement celebration, one that will punctuate the long, dry season this town has experienced.

There's a chariot in the middle of the industrial park. Its design is unconventional when compared to what one thinks of when thinking of chariots. Its body is made up of serpentine shapes crafted from obsidian-like metal pieces that are welded together seamlessly. The wheels appeared to be solid gold, or at least some similar precious metal. Visible on the front of the chariot is a single word: GLAVENI.

Philip washes the windows of the MXXX GXXXXXXX office located in the industrial park. It is a part time job, one that gives him ample opportunity to contemplate the structural code of the park and its offices. It also allows him time to mentally construct his next book. In his mind, he has the chapters planned along with the footnotes and most of the references. At some point, he will start to write everything down but not before the book is completed in his mind.

In lieu of a visit, I sent my mother a card, a simple one that has a picture of a dog on the outside and the words "THINKING OF YOU" on the inside. I know it won't satisfy her need for parasitic companionship but I had to make sure I made a small effort to counteract the inevitable accusations she will make against me during our next phone call. I want to be able to say I was thinking of her (even if the thoughts were fleeting and unflattering). I don't expect an immediate response from her. I know she is waiting for my phone call, for *me* to ask if she received the card to which she'll answer that yes, she did receive the card. But that's it. She won't say it was a nice card and she won't thank me for it. I cringe whenever I see the telephone as if it is an extension of my mother, a part of her body. I want to smash it, obliterate it, remove it from my life so I never have to speak into that suffocating abyss ever again. I can hear her voice now.

From what Philip could tell, there was no entrance to the offices of Solar Lodges Incorporated. It was supposed to be within the industrial park but no sign of it was visible. It had recently been added to the list of business he was to clean but how would he complete his custodial duties if he couldn't even find the offices? There had to be a door. What if the entrance was contained within another business as if one had swallowed the other whole? If that's the case, how will Philip find it? Would he need to be swallowed whole as well? He continues his search until he realizes it is midnight and he needs to get home.

I do not believe I am capable of leaving this room. My limbs will not obey my will to move toward the door and through the doorway. I desire to pass through the threshold (unscathed, of course) and into the parking lot where I will be visible enough to catch a ride with someone who will be willing to drop me off at the industrial park. Instead, it seems I am entrenched in warfare against my own body. Or maybe my brain is intentionally neglecting to send the appropriate commands to my body. But I want to move, goddamnit, and I want to get off this bed that smells like rotting vegetation. The ceiling above me is a mural of stains, curly multi-colored lines that harass me while I am here as prisoner. I hear the hum of the vending and ice machines outside the room. I hear coins being inserted. I hear hissing. I hear gulping. I hear the roar of rocket ships. I hear the honking of car horns. The horns are heralds of the final veil, that slithering oblivion that will eventually erase this room and erase me from the pathetic record of history.

Philip's sisters fill the barrels with milk and stack them in the basement. The five women work throughout the night and at dawn they take off their clothes and stand in the backyard away from prying eyes, protected by the thick foliage. Their milky sweat dries in the cool morning air. They squat and urinate onto the grass, into the soil, into the earth, into the insect colonies. The youngest sister walks to the house and starts to climb the ladder. Dogs bark. An owl flies out from the uppermost window of the house.

He digs in the dirt with his hands. He is looking for the burrows. He is looking for the eggs. Inside of him, his stomach is digesting toast and a round yellow pill like a miniature sun, impotent and dissolving in the galaxy of acid. Starlit, the soil glimmers on his fingers. He imagines he is a magician. A small beetle crawls across his neck and up to his ear. He is casting a spell into the earth, filling it with coiled blasphemy, all those thoughts spilling up from his guts and into his brain, out his third eye, that orb which will be stripped naked in the presence of his mother. He can hear her voice telling him to wash his hands. He will eventually obey her. The sudden hissing of water startles him. He turns around. He sees no water.

On camel bones, words are carved, feminine trickery under the guise of a recollection of youth. Owls are burned in circular pits. The black men lead the donkeys to the center where they are all swallowed by the chariot. From the front of the motel, you cannot see this nor can you see it from the highway. It is only after walking around the back and down a small hill that you could see the gathering of artifacts and animals. It is only after deciphering the words that you can check into the motel, the true one that sheds its skin.

Philip allows himself the pleasure of a drink. The alcohol will clash with his medication but he is prepared for it and therefore does not fear the ramifications. It is during this altered state that he will trample the garden and its inhabitants. It is during this altered state that he will begin to write his exegesis on the primordial development of the industrial park but only in the decaying coils of his altered mind will it ever be published.

All along the highway there are patches of woods, small fields of tall grass, and countless ditches. These ditches are of particular interest to me. I have recently documented several dozen of them in hope that I can locate the exact location of my mother's death, or rather, the location where her body was found. I do not know if she was killed there or at some other place. Because of shoddy record-keeping and frequent unnecessary landscaping projects by the city, the exact location, the exact *ditch*, is unknown at this time.

It is apparent to you that all those attending this lecture are here only because of your reputation and not your current work. They are sitting in folding chairs, anxiously waiting for a spark of controversy no matter how subtle. You are careful of the words you speak, of the implications you make, of simple hand gestures, and body language. You do not want anything you say or do to be misconstrued by this audience. You are tempted to keep talking until you are forced to stop. This way, there will be no time for questions, no time for disappointment. You have no idea if you have given them what they are expecting. You hope that is not the case. You desire nothing but the dissatisfaction of your audience.

The most I could do for you is introduce you to a woman I know who is a quasi-professional in these matters. She holds no official position, holds no degrees or certifications, but her knowledge of this topic is remarkable and unsurpassed, at least in my opinion. I might be wrong. I'm often wrong. My conclusions constantly fall short of the truth despite every effort to comb through each and every bit of evidence. I don't believe I'm wrong in this situation, though. I can introduce you to this woman and perhaps she will be able to assist you more than I have been able to, well, beyond my offer to introduce you to her.

Someone else was here in this room. I can sense it, the sense that the air is still moving, a residual presence. But who would be in this room? Who, other than me? Am I being tricked by my own hopeful emotions? Do I desire company so much that I am forcing some aspect of physicality into existence, a false trail of an imaginary guest? I cannot imagine my brain being *so* damaged as to birth such a sinister thing. I am used to isolation and am used to the emptiness of this room…but why do I feel the air slither around me, forcing me to imagine arms embracing me and eyes desiring to stare into mine? This is no way to start a morning, with dogs barking and my skin hardening in the greenish light of day while those damned owls won't stop fluttering about in the attic.

Philip is gluing photographs into an album. Each picture is placed according to an order devised by him. The pictures are of his mother and they are not being organized by date but by the emotional impact each image has on Philip. The last photo to be glued is of his mother wearing a blue dress and a large hat she often wore while working in the yard. In this picture, she is standing in a garden, one hand over her eyes to shield them from the sun and the other at her side, fist clenched. It is Philip's favorite picture and just looking at it is devastating. He closes the album and slides it back on the bookshelf where he keeps his mother's things.

The proprietor of this particular motel is named Antonio and he is telling me he has owned and operated this place for fifteen years. He had bought it from a cousin of his, a man who, according to Antonio's father, was a corrupt local politician who was later found dead from a self-inflicted gunshot wound to the abdomen. I ask Antonio if the suicide had anything to do with his political corruption and he tells me it had nothing to do with that but instead was a result of years of undiagnosed mental illness as well as drug abuse in the form of pills. I wonder if the corruption was a result of the illness and addiction or vice versa. Antonio appears apathetic to this possibility and to his cousin's life in general. I apologize for my morbid curiosity and he tells me it's quite fine, and that he's used to it.

The woman's corpse was found on the first day of summer, only two weeks after the woman filed for divorce from her husband of thirty-two years, a man who was quick to mention *he* had been the one to seek a divorce and it was only after much begging on the wife's part that he told her he would give her another chance and not seek a divorce. It was a surprise to him, the man says, that his late wife would go ahead with the filing for divorce. He has no idea who would have wanted her dead. The police have ruled him out as a suspect.

You enter the house through the side door. Instead of taking the stairs to the cellar, you take the steps up to the main floor. There you find the decapitated heads that are set on the dining room table. You take a seat at the head of the table and wait. You see the photographs on the wall, framed in driftwood. You see my face from decades ago, looking petrified as I always do when confronted with the unblinking and intrusive gaze of a camera. You see a swordfish out of water. You see a child riding a donkey. You see several thin women wrestling each other, limbs entwined, muscles flexing, mouths gaping, jaws expanding, preparing for victory. You see my husband's family, the whole lot of them, filthy and uncivilized despite their best efforts. You see my mother's wedding photo. You can see she had worn the same dress as I had on my wedding day. You can see how it fits tightly like a glove that promises nothing but agonizing disappointment. It's just like this house, a place for our pain and nothing else. I do not know if any of our family's mysteries will be solved but I do hope that you'll find peace in the belief that we have all moved on.

On the side of Highway 18 in Old Bridge, there is a certain ditch where one can find the body of a murdered woman. I did not know the woman nor did I care to. Her insignificant accomplishments were nothing in comparison to the rewards earned by her shedding the proverbial skin. Her death was something that just happened and I consider it more an act of God than an act of man or, in *my* case, a woman. She is there in the ditch for everyone to see if they would only look. If they would only open their eyes and stare at her beautiful remains... only then will I go back home.

ABOUT THE AUTHOR

Jordan Krall is the author of many books such as THE FALSE
MAGIC KINGDOM CYCLE and HUMANITY IS THE DEVIL.
He also runs DYNATOX MINISTRIES and its imprints.

www.dynatoxministries.com
www.dunhamsmanor.com

This book's story will continue in **MEDUSA** which is planned for
publication by Dunhams Manor Press in late 2016.

www.ingramcontent.com/pod-product-compliance
Lightning Source LLC
Chambersburg PA
CBHW030608130626
46552CB00006B/2699